STEP INTO READING® will help your child get there. The program offers five steps to reading success. Each step includes fun stories and colorful art or photographs. In addition to original fiction and books with favorite characters, there are Step into Reading Non-Fiction Readers, Phonics Readers and Boxed Sets, Sticker Readers, and Comic Readers—a complete literacy program with something to interest every child.

Learning to Read, Step by Step!

Ready to Read   Preschool–Kindergarten
• big type and easy words • rhyme and rhythm • picture clues
For children who know the alphabet and are eager to begin reading.

Reading with Help   Preschool–Grade 1
• basic vocabulary • short sentences • simple stories
For children who recognize familiar words and sound out new words with help.

Reading on Your Own   Grades 1–3
• engaging characters • easy-to-follow plots • popular topics
For children who are ready to read on their own.

Reading Paragraphs   Grades 2–3
• challenging vocabulary • short paragraphs • exciting stories
For newly independent readers who read simple sentences with confidence.

Ready for Chapters   Grades 2–4
• chapters • longer paragraphs • full-color art
For children who want to take the plunge into chapter books but still like colorful pictures.

STEP INTO READING® is designed to give every child a successful reading experience. The grade levels are only guides; children will progress through the steps at their own speed, developing confidence in their reading.

Remember, a lifetime love of reading starts with a single step!

CREATED BY BRITT ALLCROFT

Based on the Railway Series by The Reverend W Awdry.
© 2022 Gullane (Thomas) Limited.
Thomas the Tank Engine & Friends™ and Thomas & Friends™ are trademarks of Gullane
(Thomas) Limited. © 2022 HIT Entertainment Limited. HIT and the HIT logo are trademarks of
HIT Entertainment Limited.

Step into Reading, Random House, and the Random House colophon are registered trademarks
of Penguin Random House LLC.

Visit us on the Web!
StepIntoReading.com
rhcbooks.com
www.thomasandfriends.com

Educators and librarians, for a variety of teaching tools, visit us at RHTeachersLibrarians.com

ISBN 978-0-593-43147-4 (trade) | ISBN 978-0-593-43148-1 (library binding)

Printed in the United States of America
10 9 8 7 6 5 4 3 2 1

HiT entertainment

THOMAS
& FRIENDS

THOMAS
AND THE
ROCKET

by Nicole Johnson
based on an episode by Christopher Gentile

Random House 🏠 New York

Today is a big day!
Thomas and his friends

will bring a rocket to
Brendam Docks.

Gordon is glad.

He will bring

the top of the rocket.

Nia is glad.

She will bring the

body of the rocket.

Kana is glad.

She will bring the bottom of the rocket.

Diesel is glad.

He will bring the wings

of the rocket.

Thomas is sad.
He will bring
a small battery.

Then Thomas sees Nia.

She is stuck.

Thomas must help Nia.

He switches her track.

Gordon is stuck, too!

Thomas helps Gordon.

Cranky and the engines quickly build the rocket.

The rocket
is almost ready.

But they need the battery
to make it blast off.

Thomas hurries
to get the battery.
Uh-oh!
He hits a rock.

The battery lands
in the rocket!

There is no time to waste.

Kana hits a button.

The rocket blasts off!

The engines cheer.

Thomas saved the day.

Hooray for Thomas!